This item should be returned on or before the last date
stamped above. If not in demand it may be renewed for a
further period by personal application, by telephone, or in
writing. The author, title, above number and date due back
should be quoted.   LS/3

The Headless Ghost

Pete Johnson

Illustrated by Lucy Su

A & C Black · London

GRAFFIX

1   The Listener · Elizabeth Laird
2   Matthew's Goals · Michael Hardcastle
3   Biker · Anthony Masters
4   Captain Hawk · Jim Eldridge
5   Roller Madonnas · Bernard Ashley
6   Otherworld · Jeremy Strong
7   Bodyparts · Theresa Breslin
8   Moving the Goalposts · Rob Childs
9   The Headless Ghost · Pete Johnson
10 Laser Quest · Mick Gowar
11 Roy Kane TV Detective · Steve Bowkett
12 A Boy Like That · Tony Langham
13 Thirteen Candles · Mary Hooper
14 Lovesick · Lynda Waterhouse
15 Hero · Anthony Masters
16 Rapid · Bernard Ashley
17 Hot News · Pete Johnson
18 Goal-getter · Michael Hardcastle
19 The Cinderella Principle · Tony Langham
20 Winners and Losers · Trevor Wadlow
21 The Haunted Surfboard · Anthony Masters
22 Guard Dog · Philip Wooderson
23 The Horror of the Heights · Anthony Masters
24 Lakenham Prom · Mick Gowar
25 My Brother's a Keeper · Michael Hardcastle
26 Girl Gang · Pete Johnson
27 Mine's a Winner · Michael Hardcastle
28 Cast Away · Caroline Pitcher
29 System Shock · Liam O'Donnell
30 Respect · Bernard Ashley
31 The Kidnappers · Ursula Jones
32 Abracadabra · Alex Gutteridge
33 Ravens' Revenge · Anthony Masters
34 Hit It! · Michael Hardcastle

Reprinted 1999, 2004
First paperback edition 1998
First published 1998 in hardback by
A & C Black Publishers Ltd
37 Soho Square, London W1D 3QZ
www.acblack.com

Text copyright © 1998 Pete Johnson
Illustrations copyright © 1998 Lucy Su
Cover illustration copyright © 1998 Mike Adams

The rights of Pete Johnson and Lucy Su to be
identified as the author and illustrator respectively
of this work have been asserted by them in accordance
with the Copyright, Designs and Patents Act 1988.

ISBN 0-7136-4902-X

A CIP catalogue record for this book is available from
the British Library.

A & C Black uses paper produced with elemental chlorine-free
pulp, harvested from managed sustainable forests.

Printed in Great Britain by William Clowes Ltd., Beccles, Suffolk.

Chapter One

I looked outside.
It was getting dark.
Time for me to go.

I put on my running
shoes just in case I
had to make a quick
getaway. Then I put
on my thick jacket
to make myself look
bigger.

Grant, are you ready?

Yes, coming, Mum.

Don't tell anyone but I'm feeling a bit scared. You see, tonight I'm going on a ghost hunt with two mates, Alan and Colin, and Colin's dad, Mr Biggins. We're going to the war memorial in the old park which is supposed to be haunted - by a headless ghost.

Downstairs my mum and dad were waiting with Mr Biggins.

They all stopped talking when I appeared. I didn't know what they had been saying. But I could guess. My parents worry about me being out late at night as I'm completely deaf in my left ear and I can only hear a little - with the aid of my trusty hearing aid - in my right ear. But I can lip-read brilliantly.

Outside it was so cold my breath smoked. Colin and Alan were waiting with a girl I didn't recognise.
Hi, Grant.
I bet you're bricking it now, aren't you?
Oh yes, I'm terrified.

You haven't met my nuisance of a little sister, have you?

She insisted on coming too. She's called... something.

Hello something.

I'm not a very 'little sister', actually. I'm only one year younger than Colin. My name's Jill.

Mr Biggins hurried down the drive.

Are we ready then? Let's go to the war memorial - and see what awaits us there.

Colin and Alan started walking ahead.

I was about to follow them when Mr Biggins tapped me on the shoulder.

That's one of the worst things about being deaf, you are always being separated from your friends. Like at school, I always have to sit right at the front, far away from where my mates are.

This ghost at the war memorial. Is it always a man in uniform?

That's right, Jill, it's a man in RAF uniform; people think he's someone who was killed in World War II.

Mr Biggins went on, 'A number of people claim to have seen him standing right beside the old war memorial. They say he gives this really chilling smile, then his head starts to disappear. I'm not sure I believe them, but it's a fascinating story, isn't it?'

Mr Biggins is something of an expert on ghosts. He has even written a pamphlet, collecting together local stories. He's always going on ghost hunts. Yet, to his great disappointment, he has never seen one.

Ghosts of Past & Present

We walked the last hundred metres in silence. Colin and Alan were waiting impatiently for us by the iron gates, which led into the old park.

There was a huge park on the other side of the town and that was where everyone went now. No wonder the old park had a gloomy, neglected air. The trees were bare and still. We crunched our way through the dead leaves towards the memorial.

There were four
steps leading up to
a long grey pillar.
There were lots of
names on the pillar,
but it was too dark to
read any of them.

Jill leant forward to get a closer look.

Watch out! Don't get too close.

She immediately leapt back. Colin and Alan started laughing.

Jill's afraid the ghost's going to jump out at her.

We stared intently at Colin.

Neither did I!

That broke the atmosphere and put an end to our silence. Colin and Alan spent the next ten minutes making jokes and teasing Jill.

After a while Colin said something to me. I couldn't catch it. But I never ask anyone to repeat what they've said. They only think you're like those deaf people on TV comedies saying, 'What's that?' over and over. So I just shook my head - which is what I usually do when I don't understand the question.

Everyone looked at me in astonishment.

The next moment they were all heading for the park
gates. They were leaving me here on my own.
But I didn't want to stay here on my own.

Alan called out
something to me.
I couldn't catch
that either.
But he was
grinning, so
I grinned
back at him.

And then I was all alone. I could still run after them - say I'd changed my mind. No I couldn't, I'd let myself down if I did that. Besides, they'd only be gone for five minutes.

Chapter Two

It's amazing how long five minutes is when you're scared out of your wits. I started imagining what it must be like to be a ghost. It must be a very boring life. Except ghosts weren't alive, were they? I shivered.

The night seemed to have grown much darker. The wind was making the trees rustle. I didn't want to stay here on my own.

There was a real chill in the air now. And suddenly the war memorial was lit up. There was a grey light all around it. A shudder ran through me.

Someone was standing there. He'd just appeared out of nowhere.

It was a man, quite a young man. And he was wearing an RAF uniform.

I froze but my mind was racing. 'This is a joke,' I told myself. 'Someone is dressing up to try and scare me. Alan and Colin are probably hiding somewhere, laughing.'

Who...

I began to say: 'Who are you,' but my voice came out as little more than a squeak.

The man in the uniform just stared at me. And he was smiling. A weird smile. Then he raised his hand. He seemed to be pointing at me.

I wanted to cry out. But it was as if invisible hands had grabbed me by the throat. I couldn't move either.

Not even when I saw the top of his head vanish.

Then his eyes disappeared.

All that was left of his face was his mouth, smiling that terrible smile. Then his lips started to move.

Icy sweat trickled down my spine.

All at once I could run.

And I ran faster than I've ever run in my life.

I was certain that strange, headless creature was right behind me. I could even feel its hot breath on my neck.

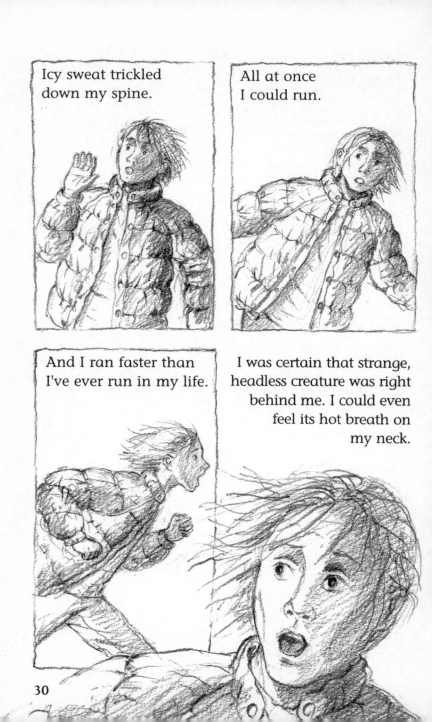

I ran straight into Mr Biggins and the others on their way back from the chip shop. They gaped at me in astonishment.

Grant, are you all right mate?

I've seen it, the Headless Ghost.

Jill dropped her bag of chips in horror.

I described what I'd seen. I couldn't stop shaking. Mr Biggins offered to take me home. But I didn't want to go.

Let's go back and see if it's still there.

We walked back to the memorial and waited for the Headless Ghost. But this time, nothing happened.

Perhaps he only does one haunting a night.

Perhaps someone imagined it. After all, you thought he was chasing after you - but he wasn't. We didn't see him anyway.

All right, I did imagine that bit. But the rest of it was true. Honestly.

I glared round at them fiercely.

35

But I knew he didn't really believe me. No-one did.
When I got home I didn't bother telling my parents.
I knew they wouldn't believe me either. My dad
would just make one of his bad jokes.

Next day was Saturday. I spent most of it writing up what I'd seen. I wanted to capture every detail. I knew it was true. It wasn't my imagination. Maybe after Mr Biggins read my report he'd believe me.

Maybe he might even go back there with me. I thought I'd be scared. I was scared. But I also wanted to see the Headless Ghost again.

That evening I took the report round to Mr Biggins' house. Mrs Biggins opened the door.

I'm sorry, Grant. He and Colin have gone to a football match with Colin's grandad.

But I'm here. Why does everyone always forget me? Anyway, do you want to come in?

Yes, okay.

Chapter Three

We switched on our
torches and headed for
the park. There was
quite a thick mist that
night. Everything
seemed disguised,
different. To be honest,
if I'd been on my own
I'd probably have
turned back. Somehow,
I didn't want to be out.
But Jill was chattering
away quite happily.
I couldn't catch
everything she said -
but I understood
enough.

The park was even quieter than the night before. The mist had practically swallowed up the war memorial. We stared up at it.

I could tell that Jill
was getting nervous.
I tried to calm her down.

I don't expect we'll see
anything tonight.

46

I wanted to go now. We shouldn't
have come here on our own.
We should have waited
for Mr Biggins. I felt
suddenly uneasy.

47

It was growing colder, much colder.

What did you say, Jill?

I didn't say anything.

I thought I'd heard someone whispering. The night was full of whisperings from another world. Now what made me think that? I had to stop winding myself up. But I couldn't help it. It felt as though there was someone nearby. Someone waiting for me.

And then my heart started to pound. For the pillar was all lit up again. I saw a figure moving out of the mist.

Jill grabbed my hand.

It was him, just as before. He was wearing an RAF uniform. His lips drew back from his face. There it was again, that chilling smile.

Then he raised his hand. He seemed to be pointing at us. Jill was clutching my hand really tightly now. A cry choked in my throat.

Grant... look...

Grant, let's go.

His lips were still smiling. But the rest of his face was blotched in grey-blackness. There were just those lips. And now they were moving. Suddenly I realised something. Why hadn't I seen it before?

Come on.

Then all at once Jill ran off into the mist.
I tore after her.

You see, right at the end his lips moved... I think he was trying to say something to us.

Yeah, like 'Go away!'. And that's what I want to do right now.

I took Jill home and made her promise not to tell anyone what we'd seen. I had some thinking to do about this.

Next morning I went back to the park again. In the daylight it didn't seem scary at all, just rather sad and forlorn. A woman was kneeling down beside the war memorial. She placed a small bunch of flowers at the foot of the pillar. Then she walked slowly away.

I looked at the flowers.
On her card she had
written:

Their names
live forever.

I gazed up at the
names engraved
on the pillar.
There were some
on the front of
the pillar, and
others round
the back.

You can't stay
away from this
place, can you?

Chapter Four

But that evening, to my surprise, Jill turned up at my house.

Perhaps I won't be scared this time. I can't be out too late, though, it's school tomorrow.

Let's hope he turns up on time then.

It was a brighter night this evening, and the sky was teeming with stars. We gazed up at the pillar.

Perhaps we could call out all these names and see if he answers.

Go on then.

I was only joking.

61

We stood quietly for a few minutes.

Ghosts can't really do anything to you, can they? They can walk through you, I suppose, which wouldn't be very nice, but...

Sssh, look.

The pillar was once again bathed in grey light, and then, suddenly, there he was. The young airman.

He was smiling at us. Only tonight his smile didn't seem scary at all. A little strange, perhaps, but then it's probably quite hard to smile when you're a ghost.

He looked straight into my eyes as if he was trying to see what I was thinking. He pointed his hand forward. Then his face started to vanish.

Jill clung on to my arm.

I still hate this bit.

But I leaned forward eagerly.
For his lips were moving;
and now I could make out
what he was saying:

Keep away from here. You are in great danger.

What?

That's what he said.

But how do you know? I couldn't understand a word.

I can lip-read, can't I.

Oh yes, I forgot. But what does he mean, 'great danger'?

I shook my head. By now the ghost had vanished again.

Look, we've got to figure this out. Each time the ghost appears, smiles, points at us.

'Only he might not be pointing at us,' said Jill. 'He might be pointing at something buried around here... like, well, it would be great if it were treasure. But that wouldn't explain why he said, 'You are in great danger.'

So it's probably something very bad like...

But neither Jill's parents nor mine were in the mood to listen to us. They were too busy being angry. You see, Mr Biggins had rung up my home to speak to Jill. When he found out she wasn't there he began to panic. He got my parents worked up as well. When we got home they were all waiting for us.

Look, we're really sorry for not telling you before. But this is urgent.

Then Jill and I told them everything we'd seen. My parents were very sceptical.

Mr Biggins seemed to almost believe us.

Well, I don't know. Hmm. It's a most unusual story, of course, but maybe... Hmm. I wonder.

Then he made us tell him the whole story again, while he wrote down everything we said.

Chapter Five

For the next few days neither Jill nor I were allowed out at night. But we were allowed to help Mr Biggins in his research.

First we must try to identify your ghost.

So we went to the library and looked through some old local papers from World War II. We were ages searching for him.

That really shocked me. You don't imagine ghosts being young, do you? I felt sad for him. And now he had a name. He was called James Leigh.

Each day Jill and I met in the old park.

I don't think my dad's doing anything at all. And that bomb could go off at any time.

But then one Friday we found the whole park was cordoned off. And there were police everywhere. It seemed Mr Biggins had listened to us after all. He had been visiting the library to check through some old local papers from World War II. That evening all the people living near the park had to leave their homes and spend the night in our school. I reckon that's nearly as bad as being bombed.

The following day it was headline news in the local paper:

Experts reckoned the bomb had been dropped there in World War II and never found. They said it could have exploded at any time.

There were pictures of Jill and me in the paper too. We were called 'brave' and 'clever', for although lots of people had seen the Headless Ghost, none of them had understood what he was trying to say. But then I doubt if any of them could lip-read.

Colin was so impressed by Jill he was nice to her for a whole morning. And yesterday this couple in the town recognised me and asked if they could shake my hand. But it wasn't my hand they should've been shaking. Not that I could imagine them ever shaking hands with a ghost.

A week later, Jill and I went back to the war
memorial. We both had flowers.
Mine was a wreath of poppies.